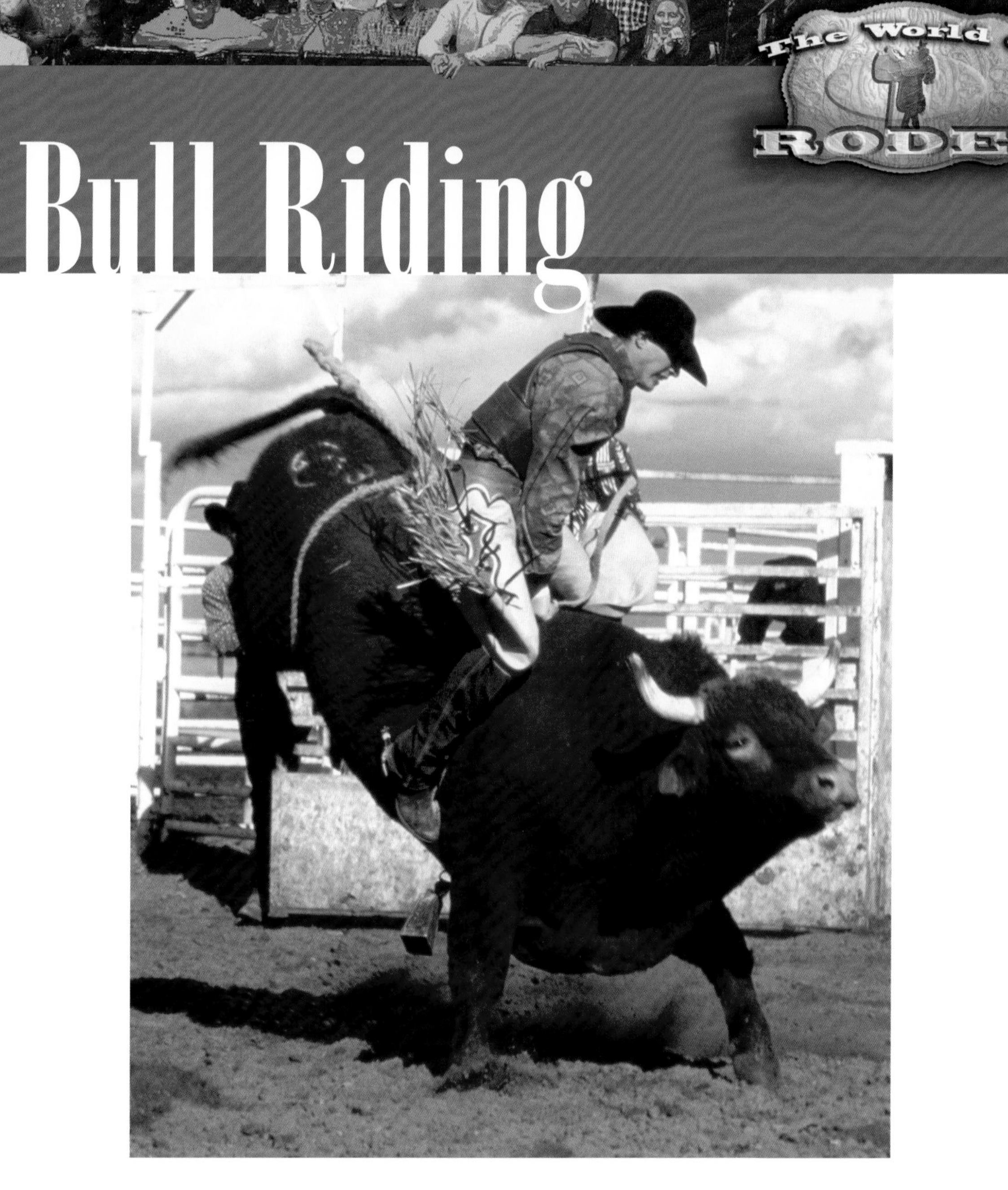

Bull Riding

Jane and Jessica Kubke

The Rosen Publishing Group, Inc., New York

Published in 2006 by The Rosen Publishing Group, Inc.
29 East 21st Street, New York, NY 10010

First Edition

Library of Congress Cataloging-in-Publication Data

Kubke, Jane.
Bull riding/Jane and Jessica Kubke.—1st ed.
p. cm.—(The world of rodeo)
Includes bibliographical references and index.
ISBN 1-4042-0544-6 (library binding)
1. Bull riding—Juvenile literature. I. Kubke, Jessica. II. Title. III. Series.
GV1834.45.B84K83 2006
791.8'4--dc22

2005017390

Manufactured in the United States of America

On the cover: During a rodeo's bull-riding competition, a rider attempts to stay on a bucking Brahman bull for the full eight seconds required to receive a score.

Contents

	Introduction	4
Chapter 1	The Roots of Rodeo	6
Chapter 2	The Making of a Bull Rider	15
Chapter 3	Bull Riding: The Basics	21
Chapter 4	Judging and Scoring	29
	Conclusion	36
	List of Champions	37
	Glossary	40
	For More Information	42
	For Further Reading	44
	Bibliography	45
	Index	47

Introduction

Among the classic rodeo sports, bull riding is the lone event that has no origins in practical ranch work. There has only ever been one reason for cowboys to climb on the backs of bulls—to see if it can be done. It is the most dangerous and the most punishing of all rodeo events, and it is no accident that it is also the most popular among fans. The electrifying spectacle of a 150-pound (68 kilogram) man trying to ride a kicking, spinning, writhing 2,000-pound (907 kg) bull for eight seconds while using only one hand to hang on keeps spectators glued to their seats.

The majority of bull-riding events take place at rodeos in the continental United States, but bulls are also ridden at rodeos in Canada, Mexico, Brazil, Argentina, New Zealand, and Australia. While American cowboys have long dominated bull riding, cowboys from other countries have risen to the top of the sport in recent years. The last decade has seen a dramatic restructuring of professional competition, and bull riding has been recast as an extreme sport, gaining it a new and expanded following.

In this book, you will learn about the men who ride bulls and about the history, technique, and judging of bull riding.

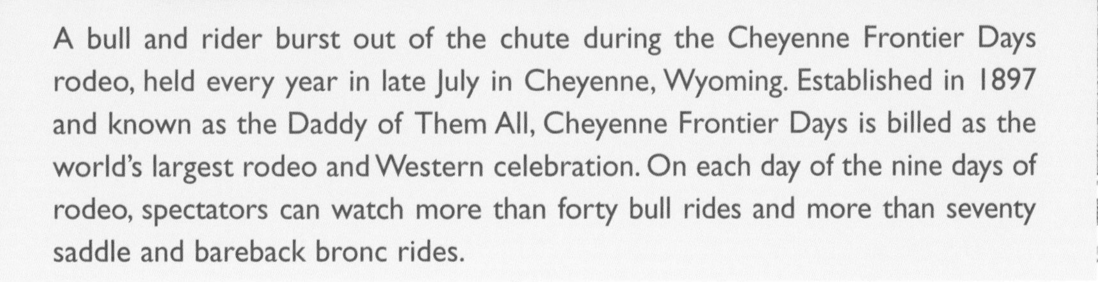

A bull and rider burst out of the chute during the Cheyenne Frontier Days rodeo, held every year in late July in Cheyenne, Wyoming. Established in 1897 and known as the Daddy of Them All, Cheyenne Frontier Days is billed as the world's largest rodeo and Western celebration. On each day of the nine days of rodeo, spectators can watch more than forty bull rides and more than seventy saddle and bareback bronc rides.

CHAPTER 1

THE ROOTS OF RODEO

The tradition of rodeo as we know it today is rooted in the history of ranching in the late nineteenth century, when working cowboys entertained themselves by challenging one another to take part in informal competitions. These competitive challenges were variations on the duties that cowboys performed in the course of their daily ranch work, such as roping calves and riding unbroken horses.

Yet rodeo was not simply a display of practical livestock management. It was also an entertaining, even thrilling spectacle. On a working cattle ranch, it never becomes necessary to hop on the back of cattle and ride them. Cattle are herded and driven, not ridden. This did not prevent some thrill-seeking cowboys from giving it a try, however, and the first recorded instance of cowboys riding cattle was in Cheyenne, Wyoming, in 1872. The Navajo were also known for riding cattle for as long as they could hang on.

This showmanship aspect of rodeo was incorporated into traveling Western-themed shows, such as Buffalo Bill Cody's Wild West show and the Miller brothers' 101 Ranch Show. These were lucrative businesses that were part history lesson and part circus entertainment, built upon the showcasing of frontier-flavored thrills and spills for paying audiences across the United States. By the 1880s, Buffalo Bill Cody's Wild West show had added wild steer riding to its program.

FRANK LESLIE'S
ILLUSTRATED
NEWSPAPER

No. 1,703.—Vol. LXVI.] NEW YORK—FOR THE WEEK ENDING MAY 5, 1888. [Price, 10 Cents.

COWBOY LIFE.—RIDING A YEARLING.
From a Photo. by C. D. Kirkland, Cheyenne.—See Page 182.

The cover image of an 1888 issue of *Frank Leslie's Illustrated Newspaper* depicts a cowboy riding a yearling bull (a one-year-old bull) as his fellow ranch hands cheer him on. Frank Leslie was an England-born publisher of magazines and newspapers in the United States. His *Illustrated Newspaper* was the first successful illustrated weekly periodical in the country.

The first rodeo to award cash prizes was held in Pecos, Texas, in 1883, followed by a rodeo in Prescott, Arizona, in 1888. Thereafter, rodeos gradually began replacing the Wild West show. Cheyenne Frontier Days (in Wyoming)—the so-called Daddy of Them All—was first held in 1897. The Pendleton Round-Up (in Oregon) and the Calgary Stampede (in Alberta, Canada) were first held in 1910 and 1912, respectively. None of these early rodeos included bull riding, but two-handed steer riding was first added as a professional rodeo event at Prescott Frontier Days in 1913.

RODEO BECOMES ORGANIZED

Up until the end of the 1920s, rodeos were independently produced and promoted. With the creation of the Rodeo Association of America (RAA), however, rodeo rules and events began to be standardized and competition became better organized. The RAA declared the riding of mature bulls an official rodeo event in 1929. In the same year, the RAA began naming national champions in each rodeo event, using a point system based on earnings.

While rodeo was growing in popularity among spectators in the 1930s, cowboys did not necessarily feel that the prize money they were receiving reflected their efforts. Rodeo was extremely dangerous and required almost constant, exhausting, and expensive travel. In addition, each cowboy had to pay an entry fee for the privilege of competing in a rodeo. Meanwhile, rodeo promoters and organizers were bringing in lots of cash thanks to the large crowds willing to pay for such exciting entertainment. Yet the earnings top competitors were receiving

The opening ceremonies of Cheyenne Frontier Days is captured in this 1910 panoramic photograph. Former U.S. president Theodore Roosevelt can be seen standing on the fourth step of the flag-draped gazebo in front of the grandstands. In the inset photo, rodeo cowboy Verne Elliott rides a buffalo. Following injuries suffered at the 1910 Frontier Days rodeo, Elliott retired from rodeo participation and became a stock contractor, supplying rodeos with livestock for competitors to ride and rope. He also introduced bull riding to the Forth Worth Rodeo in the 1920s and developed side-release chutes in 1927.

for their dangerous work were barely allowing them to make ends meet. Competitors thought it was particularly unfair that some rodeos did not pay back entry fees as part of the winners' purses. Their dissatisfaction came to a head during the 1936 Boston Garden Rodeo, when sixty-one disgruntled cowboys walked out, causing the rodeo promoter to relent finally and offer the cowboys more prize money.

Following this event, the Cowboys Turtle Association was formed to look after the interests of cowboys, not only in terms of winners' payouts, but also with respect to uniformity of rules and safe conditions for the cowboys and the livestock at all rodeos. They used the name "turtle" because, though they had been slow to organize themselves, once they were committed, they stuck their necks out. In 1945, the Cowboys Turtle Association's name was changed to the Rodeo Cowboys Association, and in 1975 the name was changed again to the Professional Rodeo Cowboys Association (PRCA), which still represents professional cowboys today.

Brahman bulls, also called zebu, like the one shown above, are native to India, where they are considered sacred by Hindus. Brahman bulls are very large, weighing 1,600 to 2,000 pounds (726 to 907 kilograms). The characteristic hump over their shoulders is formed by fat and cartilage. The loose, hanging skin at the neck is also typical of the breed. Despite its size and weight, the Brahman bull is nimble, which is why it has become so popular among rodeo bull riders who love a good challenge. In North America, the Brahman bull has been crossbred with European cattle, so very few rodeo bulls are purebred Brahmans.

The best interests of both female and younger rodeo competitors were soon looked after by similar member organizations. The Women's Professional Rodeo Association (WPRA) was created in 1948, and the National Intercollegiate Rodeo Association (NIRA) and the National High School Rodeo Association (NHSRA) were both created in 1949.

THE BULLS

While rodeo was evolving with respect to the organization and protection of cowboys, the event of bull riding truly came of age as a spectator sport in the 1950s, when the Brahman cattle strain, first introduced into the breeding of bucking bulls in the late 1920s, came to predominate among the stock of rodeo bulls. Brahmans had been imported into the United States from India from as early as the mid-nineteenth century and were large, tough, hardy, and flexible animals. They were initially bred with longhorn cattle, which were notorious for having nasty dispositions. The crossing of the two breeds produced an incredibly active and dynamic bucking bull, and by the 1950s, Brahman bull riding was a standard event in most rodeos. Brahmans have since been crossed with almost all breeds of cattle, from Jerseys to Charolais.

The new Brahman-cross bulls were bigger, harder-bucking, and very popular with audiences, yet these assets were also liabilities. Brahman bulls feared neither man nor beast. In the arena, they were as likely to charge horses as they were the cowboys they had bucked off, so it was too dangerous to have pick-up men on horseback to help riders get off the bulls when their rides were over. Bull riders needed help, and the humble rodeo clown came to their rescue.

RODEO CLOWNS AND BULLFIGHTERS

Funny men had long been a part of rodeos, performing acts and telling jokes while there was a lull in the action. But with the aggressive new bull breeds rampaging around the arena, many bull riders would not participate in the event if rodeo clowns were not present to help distract the bulls after the cowboys' rides, giving them a

As the riding of Brahman bulls became standard in more and more rodeos around the country, rodeo clowns were joined by bullfighters *(above)* who protected riders from increasingly powerful and active bulls, while rodeo clowns still amused spectators. To help bullfighters distract charging bulls—and amuse the crowds—rodeo clowns often rolled inner tubes or barrels at them or taunted the bulls with Spanish bullfighting capes.

chance to get off the arena floor and back behind the safety of the surrounding fences. The increased risk and danger of dealing with the feisty Brahmans drove some rodeo clowns to leave the profession. The ones who stayed had the difficult task of distracting the bull by exposing themselves to mortal danger, while still making the effort look entertaining to the audience.

The rodeo clown's main responsibility remains entertaining the crowd between bull rides. As bulls have become ever more dangerous, trained bullfighters have replaced rodeo clowns where protecting bull riders is concerned. The rodeo clown still exists, but he is now called the barrel man. He must never stray too far from a barrel placed on the arena floor that he can jump into if a bull charges him.

In contemporary bull riding, the real protecting of bull riders is done by two bullfighters. These highly trained athletes also dress as clowns, with painted faces and tattered clothes, but for them protecting bull riders is no laughing matter.

Founded in 1992 by twenty bull riders, the athlete-owned and athlete-operated PBR has succeeded in showcasing bull riding as a wildly popular professional sport independent of rodeo. It has gained recognition for its 700 members as mainstream professional athletes.

COMPETITION TODAY

Although bull riding had developed a loyal and enthusiastic audience at rodeos throughout the 1970s and 1980s, televised coverage of rodeo remained limited. Usually, only a small number of very high-profile rodeos were broadcast each year on the major networks. As a consequence of a relatively small audience and limited corporate sponsorship, neither the winners' purses nor the sport's audience was growing. With about 750 PRCA-sanctioned rodeos held per year, good bull riders spent the bulk of their lives on the road, racing thousands of miles between hundreds of rodeos widely scattered across North America every season. Rodeo cowboys could spend up to 75 percent of their earnings on travel alone. Riding bulls was not only a dangerous way to make a living; it was also a hard way to make a living.

The entire tradition of rodeo competition was changed radically by a group of twenty bull riders in 1992, with the creation of Pro Bull Riders (PBR). The PBR's beginnings—not unlike those of the Cowboys' Turtle Association—lay in the dissatisfaction of top bull riders with their earnings. They felt that they were earning too little in exchange for the danger to which they exposed themselves, especially

The Women

Many women held starring roles in Wild West shows and competed against men in early rodeos, but they were gradually excluded from most rodeo competitions. Today, women dominate rodeo's barrel-racing and pole-bending events, and often compete in calf-roping, team-roping, cutting, and bronc-riding events. While they are not numerous, some women compete in bull-riding events today. In WPRA-sanctioned rodeos, women ride for six rather than eight seconds.

in comparison with cowboys in far safer rodeo events, and with professional athletes in other sports. The bull riders reasoned that the extreme danger and excitement of bull riding was what most rodeo fans came to see, yet they were splitting the purse equally with the cowboys in tamer roping and riding events. Bull riding had as much or more appeal than any other televised professional sport, they believed, so there was no reason they couldn't strike out on their own, generate a huge television audience, and attract enough corporate sponsorship to create larger rewards—in the form of cash prizes—for their dangerous efforts.

Gambling on the PBR paid off, and the bull riders haven't looked back. In 1994, the PBR purse was $250,000, and by 2004, it had grown to $9.66 million. In the same period, its membership grew from about twenty bull riders competing in eight events to more than 700 competing in almost thirty events. (In contrast, in 2004, the PRCA had more than 6,000 members competing in 671 rodeos, with total prize money of $35.5 million.) Today, PBR events draw huge live and television audiences on a thirty-one-stop tour. The PRCA quickly realized the undeniable appeal of bull riding–only events and now stages a similar ten-event series called Xtreme Bulls. Bull riders now have a choice of competing in PBR or PRCA events, and some cowboys compete in both and are members of both associations.

CHAPTER 2

THE MAKING OF A BULL RIDER

Bucking bulls are violent and unpredictable. They are given to spinning, leaping, and kicking abruptly, and they are extremely powerful animals. Riding them requires strength, balance, good upper-body control, strong legs, good coordination, quick reflexes, and flexibility. The optimal build for a bull rider is roughly 5 feet 8 inches (1.7 meters) tall and about 150 pounds (68 kg). This is because a smaller, more compact body means the bull rider's center of gravity is sitting low on the bull's back, making the body more stable and less affected by the bull's whipsawing motion.

Having the ideal bull rider physique doesn't necessarily make someone an ideal bull rider, though. The 1970 world bull-riding champ and bull-riding school director, Gary Leffew, speaking to Trevor Thieme of *Men's Health*, claims that "bull riding is 80 percent mental and 20 percent talent." Certainly there are few sports that demand more mental skills—courage, single-mindedness, tolerance of pain, and the elusive quality that cowboys call "try"—than bull riding. Bull riders have the shortest careers of all cowboys; they get bucked off more often than they score a qualified (completed) ride, and they face the odds of a serious wreck on one out of about every fifteen rides. "Try" is that little bit of extra effort that keeps the cowboy on the bull's back for eight seconds, even when the odds are so heavily stacked against him and in favor of the beast.

Lee Ferris, also known as the "Canada Kid," rides a bucking steer during a bull-riding event at the Calgary Stampede. Ferris was part of the rodeo circuit in the 1930s, during the heyday of the renowned bull riders John and Frank Schneider, Smoky Snyder, and Dick Griffith. He participated in some of the era's biggest and most important rodeos, including the Stampede and Cheyenne Frontier Days.

EARLY CHAMPIONS

Throughout the 1930s, bull riding was dominated by three tough Californians: John and Frank Schneider, and five-time world champion Smokey Snyder. Professional bull riding's first widely recognized star was Dick Griffith, a talented cowboy with a showman's flair, from Fort Worth, Texas. Griffith's first career had been as a trick rider, and he often appeared in the arena dressed in a tuxedo to the delight of the audience. He won four consecutive world titles from 1939 through 1942.

Griffith's successor was Ken Roberts, who grew up in a rodeo family in Kansas. Roberts and his sister were both performers in Clyde Miller's Wild West show before Roberts became a professional rodeo cowboy. His trademark laid-back style won him three consecutive world titles from 1943 through 1945.

The ability of young men with no ranching background to break into and succeed in bull riding was demonstrated by the event's defining rivalry in the 1950s, between Harry Tompkins and Jim Shoulders. Harry Tompkins was an amateur inventor who grew up in upstate New York and got his professional rodeo start at the Madison Square Garden Rodeo in New York City. He packed as many as seventy-five rodeos into a season, which was a huge number for the time, given that the great interstate highways were not yet built and commercial aviation was still in its infancy. Tompkins was one of the first cowboys to get his pilot's license so that he could fly himself to rodeos.

Shoulders, Tompkins's principal rival, was a mechanic's son from Henryetta, Oklahoma. Physically, the odds were against a 6-feet-tall (1.8 m) man like Jim Shoulders making it as a bull rider. Despite not conforming to the classic bull-riding physique, Shoulders dominated because it is grit and determination that ultimately make the bull rider. Shoulders won world titles as all-around cowboy and bareback bronco rider in addition to his seven bull-riding titles. He is the only cowboy in history to win the world bull-riding title six consecutive times, from 1954 through 1959. His total of sixteen world championships is a record that still stands today.

Jim Shoulders *(above)* stands amidst his collection of championship saddles and trophies. Shoulders competed professionally in bull riding and bareback riding from 1945 to 1970. He placed in both events in his final rodeo at the age of forty-two.

THE YOUNG GUNS

The 1980s gave rise to a new generation of top-notch bull riders who were friends, traveling companions, and competitors. This group included Tuff Hedeman, Lane Frost, Cody Lambert, Clint Branger, Jim Sharp, and Ty Murray.

By the time these cowboys had risen to the top of their sport, the lifestyle of the professional cowboy had evolved. This group of elite bull riders was better known for traveling by plane and arriving at rodeos just in time for their event than for the lonesome crisscrossing of North America in beat-up pick-up trucks that cowboys had traditionally done. Tuff Hedeman once claimed that he had arrived

Leading competitors in the Tuff Hedeman Bull Riding Challenge line up for an introduction to the audience at the Will Rogers Memorial Coliseum in Fort Worth, Texas, on March 13, 1998. Tuff Hedeman is a three-time PRCA bull-riding world champion and one-time PBR world champion. After retiring from bull riding, he became president of PBR and now produces a five-event Tuff Hedeman Championship Challenge Bull Riding Series. Each of the five events in the series is approved by the PRCA and offers $100,000 in prize money. Points earned in the series count toward the Wrangler National Finals Rodeo.

so late to every rodeo one season that he had not yet heard the national anthem played at a single one.

By the 1980s, rodeo prize money was increasing, the competition was getting stiffer, and riding bulls for a living was increasingly perilous. Men from all walks of life continued to be drawn to the perils and promise of this dangerous and thrilling event. The first African American world champion bull rider was Charles Sampson, who grew up in Los Angeles, California, and got interested in rodeo when he started riding ponies and steers at a nearby stable. He won the gold buckle in bull

Jesse Guillory *(far left)*, manager of the Bill Pickett Invitational Rodeo, assigns bulls to riders for the rodeo's upcoming bull-riding events in Beaumont, Texas, in June 2005. The rodeo is named after Bill Pickett, an African American cowboy who was born in 1870 and is credited with inventing bulldogging (wrestling steers to the ground by grabbing their horns and twisting their necks). The Bill Pickett Invitational Rodeo is a touring rodeo for African American cowboys that was begun in 1984 as the Bill Pickett Black Rodeo. Today it draws thousands of spectators to its rodeos held across the country, from Washington, D.C., to Los Angeles, California, and many towns and cities in between.

riding in 1982. In the course of his long, injury-riddled career, Sampson broke both jaws, lost numerous teeth, had an ear sliced off, broke many bones in his face, and broke his leg seven times. Despite this catalog of injuries, Charles Sampson continued to get on bulls for sixteen years. "For me it took me overcoming the fear, overcoming the idea that that bull is going to kill me!" he said (as quoted in the television broadcast *California Heartland Special Edition*).

On some terrible occasions, the bulls have killed the cowboys who have tried to ride them. Lane Frost was the 1987 world champion and had made

A statue of Lane Frost riding a bucking bull adorns the grounds of the Cheyenne Frontier Days Old West Museum in Cheyenne, Wyoming. The statue is a memorial to Frost, who was killed on July 30, 1989, at Cheyenne Frontier Days. Lane had just completed a ride that earned him a score of 85, good enough for a third-place finish. Following his dismount, Frost was on all fours when the bull turned suddenly and hooked him in the left side, breaking a rib, which may in turn have severed an artery and resulted in heart failure. Frost was only twenty-five years old.

rodeo history in 1988 by staying on the ultimate eliminator bull, Red Rock, who had remained unridden in 311 outings. It was a huge loss to the entire rodeo community when Frost made a qualified ride on a bull called Taking Care of Business at Cheyenne Frontier Days in 1989, and, following his dismount, was hooked by the bull's horn. The horn broke one of Frost's ribs, and the sharp ends of bone probably tore an artery, causing irreparable damage to the cowboy's heart. Frost, who was only twenty-five, died of his injuries.

"I know I'll continue to ride because that's what I do," Cody Lambert said in an interview following Lane Frost's death (as quoted on the Lane Frost Quotes page of the Official Lane Frost Tribute Web site). "But when someone who's one of the best, if not the best ever, has a perfect ride and gets off in good shape and then gets killed, it makes you realize how dangerous it is." Brent Thurman, Lari Sluggett, and Glen Keeley are some of the other young cowboys who have also lost their lives riding bulls.

CHAPTER 3

BULL RIDING: THE BASICS

In terms of rules and required equipment, bull riding is the simplest of rodeo events. To score, the bull rider must ride the bull for eight seconds. He may use only one hand to hang on; he may not touch the bull, himself, or any part of the equipment with his free hand. Stripped down to the essentials, the only particular equipment that the bull rider requires is the bull rope that goes around the bull and to which the cowboy holds on, as well as a glove for his riding hand. The glove gives the rider a better grip on the rope while also preventing rope burns.

The bull rope is a flat-woven rope with a loop on one end and a tail on the other. Closer to the loop end of the rope is a leather-reinforced handhold into which the cowboy's riding hand fits. Just before or immediately after the bull is led into the chute, the bull rider drops the tail of his bull rope over the bull's back and uses a wire hook to catch the tail end of the rope. He then threads the tail end through the loop so that the rope loosely encircles the bull by passing over its shoulders and behind its front legs. The tail end of the rope is then free and will be laid across the bull rider's palm to take the wrap when the cowboy is in the chute preparing for his ride.

A flank strap, used in both bronc and bull riding, is a sheepskin-lined strap that fits around the bull's hindquarters and makes the bull buck harder and extend its back legs farther when it kicks. While the flank strap irritates the bull and provokes it to kick to try to get it off, it is not very tight and it doesn't cause the bull any

A bull rider stretches out before competing in the annual Houston Livestock Show and Rodeo in Houston, Texas. The Livestock Show and Rodeo, a three-week-long event, attracts about 2 million visitors. Millions of dollars in proceeds are contributed to college scholarships for Texas students.

harm. The flank strap has already been loosely fastened around the bull's hindquarters when the bull is run into the chute. It is tightened just before the chute opens. Its quick-release buckle is released by a bullfighter or a livestock handler when the ride is over. No longer chafed by the strap, the bull is usually pacified, making it easier to herd it out of the arena without any harm coming to cowboys, bullfighters, or rodeo clowns.

PREPARATION

There are as many rituals related to ride preparation as there are bull riders. However, most bull riders will rosin their ropes; secure their boots with leather straps; don chaps and whatever additional safety equipment they use; and put on their riding gloves, which are also tightened with leather straps. Once fully dressed and ready, many bull riders do some stretching or other form of warm-up.

Once the bull is in the chute, the cowboy climbs up the bars of the chute. He then straddles the bull with his feet still resting on the bars on either side of the chute so that he is atop the bull, but his full weight is not yet resting on it. The bull rider keeps himself as far back as possible, out of the range of the bull's horns. A few other cowboys will be standing beside the chute, ready to reach in and pull the bull rider to safety if the bull acts up or begins bucking while still in the chute. Being in the chute can be a dangerous time for the bull rider, as the bull's weight can pin the bull rider's legs against the bars of the chute, crushing them. In addition, if a bull bucks, it's easy for a cowboy to be thrown against the metal or wood sides of the chute, causing potentially serious injury.

The bull rider then adjusts his rope so that the handhold is where he wants it atop the bull, and another cowboy will help him pull the rope tightly, straight upward. The bull rider rubs his rosined glove up and down on the taut rope in order to make the rosin tacky (sticky) where he will make his wrap. Then he slips his gloved hand into the handhold with his palm facing upward and his fingers pointing in the direction of the bull's head. He lays the rosined rope tail across his palm and closes his fingers over it, while he wraps the tail of the rope around the back of his wrist, lays it across his palm again, and makes a closed fist. Some bull riders then pass the tail back between the ring and pinkie fingers.

A bull rider has mounted a bull and prepared the wrap in this photograph taken moments before the chute opened and the wild ride began. Bull riders usually wear a glove only on the hand that grips the bull rope. It is usually made of thick but supple yellow leather, offering protection from rope burn while also allowing flexibility for a better grip on the rope. The glove is usually taped to the hand to prevent the bull's force and the rope's friction from tearing it off during a ride.

The wrap must be tight but still easy to release by pulling on the rope tail. If the wrap doesn't release easily, a cowboy may fall off a bucking bull while his hand remains caught. The result is that he will get dragged around the arena by the bull and perhaps caught under its kicking and stamping hooves. Some riders, seeking any advantage that will help them better hold on for eight seconds, take their chances and opt for a more secure, less easily released wrap. This is known as the suicide wrap.

A young bull rider waits for the chute gate to be pulled open and his ride to begin at the National Little Britches Rodeo finals at Penrose Stadium and Equestrian Center in Colorado Springs, Colorado, in August 2002. The annual finals rodeo is a weeklong event, drawing hundreds of competitors from across the United States, ranging from ages five to eighteen. Little Britches Rodeo is the oldest national junior rodeo association in the country.

The Bulls

The livelihood of stock contractors—people who provide rodeos with the calves, broncs, and bulls required for the various events—depends on the good health and strong performances of their bulls. They won't get much repeat business from rodeos if the bulls they provide are sick or lethargic. For this reason, stock contractors try to limit the time the bulls spend traveling. Some make a point of only driving bulls at night, when it is cool. To avoid injury, illness, and exhaustion, most adult bulls only buck at rodeos twenty or thirty times a year.

THE RIDE

When the cowboy is satisfied with his wrap, he settles his weight down on the bull's back, puts his feet down by the bull's sides, and moves his body forward so that he is tight up against his handhold. He nods, the chute is opened, and all predictability ends. The bull will buck, spin, jump in the air, kick its legs to one side (known as a body roll), and do anything else it thinks might get the cowboy off its back. The cowboy tries to match the bull's moves without losing his seated position.

The bull rider keeps his riding arm slightly flexed, while pushing his fist into the bull's back. He uses his free arm for balance and tries to keep his center of gravity right on the middle of the bull, all the while trying to hug tightly to the bull with his legs and feet. The bull rider's mantra is: "lose your feet, lose your seat." Like other rough-stock cowboys, bull riders wear spurs, but they dull the rowels and fix them so they don't rotate, which helps them to grip on to bulls using their legs and feet.

Bull riders are required to have bells attached to their bull rope that hang on the underside of the bull. Not only does the clanging and banging of the bells irritate the bull, but the weight of them makes the rope fall to the ground once the wrap is released. This helps ensure that the bull will calm down somewhat

This bull is demonstrating some of the reactions that typically lead to a high-scoring ride. He is simultaneously bucking and spinning, greatly increasing the degree of difficulty the bull rider faces in trying to stay on the bull for a full eight seconds. The rider's technique, on the other hand, may lead to either a low score or a no score. His riding arm appears to be straightening out. His free arm is close to and perhaps touching his body. The bull appears to be spinning left, away from the right-handed cowboy's hand. Finally, the rider's center of gravity appears to be pulling back and away from the middle of the bull's back.

once the cowboy is off its back and trying to exit the arena safely. In addition to the bells and the rider on his back, the bull is also aggravated by the bullfighter, who will taunt the bull in an effort to get him to buck more and give a better ride, resulting in more points for the rider.

By spinning, the bull is trying to get the rider off its back by centripetal motion (a spinning, circular motion). The bull rider's natural tendency is to resist being slung outward by leaning into the spin. If a bull rider leans into the spin too much and has too much flex in his arm, however, he winds up getting sucked into what bull riders call the well. This is very dangerous, because in the well there is a strong chance that the rider will be hooked, trampled, or otherwise hurt by the bull. If a bull rider allows his riding arm to straighten out, it loses its function as a shock absorber and he tends to slip back, away from his riding hand, a position from which he is easily bounced off the back of the bull.

While the traditional cowboy hat offers some protection to a bull rider's head, cushioning the impact of a fall to the arena's dirt floor or a stray kick of a bull's hoof, it will not guard the skull from the more dangerous and violent trauma that a trampling bull can inflict. An increasing number of riders are wearing not only helmets to protect their heads, but also face masks like the one shown above to protect their faces and jaws.

Bull riders have the easiest time if the bull spins "into" their hand, which means that a bull spins to the right for a right-handed cowboy and to the left for a left-handed cowboy. If the opposite occurs and a bull spins "away" from a bull rider's hand, it is harder for the cowboy to keep control in the spin and, if he loses his seat, it is very likely that he will be thrown off the bull but with his hand still in the wrap. This is known as being hung up, and it is an extremely dangerous position to be in. Once hung up, the bull rider cannot release his wrap himself. As a result, he is often dragged around the arena, hanging by one arm, until one of the bullfighters gets close enough to release his wrap for him.

If the bull rider stays on for eight seconds and the horn blows, signaling that he has completed his ride, it is safest to wait until the bullfighters have the bull's attention before pulling his wrap and jumping to the ground. This way the bull is distracted and charges the bullfighters rather than the bull rider. As soon as he is on the ground, the bull rider will try to run a safe distance away from the bull toward a spot in the arena where he can climb to safety up the bars of the chute or the fence if the bull charges him.

SAFETY EQUIPMENT

Over the past few decades, a number of innovations have made bull riding safer for cowboys. Bull rider Cody Lambert first designed and wore the Kevlar vest that most bull riders now wear. Its design is based on bulletproof vests of the kind worn by police officers. The Kevlar—a lightweight, flexible, but extremely strong fiber—absorbs the shock of a bull's foot, head, or horns hitting the bull rider's torso. It spreads the impact over a wider area and helps prevent serious injury. In PBR competition, vests are mandatory.

Many bull riders also wear a mouth guard, a brace to support their necks during a ride's typically rough jerking action, and a helmet to protect the head against falls and trampling hooves. While many bull riders don't like the additional weight of helmets and the way they can block their vision when riding, they will nevertheless often wear one when they are recovering from injury or have drawn a bull that is notorious for jerking cowboys down and causing a collision between the rider's and bull's heads.

CHAPTER 4

JUDGING AND SCORING

As with other riding events in rodeo, the maximum score that can be awarded for a bull ride is 100. Only bull riders who stay on the bulls for the full eight seconds and keep their free hands clear of their equipment and the bulls receive points. Those who are bucked off get zero, as do those who stay on for eight seconds but touch themselves or the bulls with their free hands. Half of the score is determined by the performance of the cowboy, and the other half is determined by the performance of the bull he rides. Typically, two judges each award a score from 1 to 25 for the bull, and two other judges each award a score of 1 to 25 for the cowboy. The four scores are added together for a possible total of 100.

The judges who score the bull's performance watch to see how difficult the bull is to ride. Changes in direction that are abrupt and frequent—spinning, kicking, body rolls, and being droppy—make a bull more difficult to ride and will earn the rider a higher score. A difficult, high-scoring bull is referred to as "rank." The power and speed the bull demonstrates can also boost the cowboy's point total.

While a bull rider has beat the odds simply by staying on a bull until the horn sounds, the judges have higher standards to consider than mere completion of the ride. They score the bull rider by gauging whether he is demonstrating control and correct body position as he matches the movements of the bull without losing his seat. If the bull rider manages to spur his bull during the brief ride, he can be awarded extra points.

Wayne Motes is bucked off his bull at a rough stock competition in Alamorosa, New Mexico, on March 10, 2002, receiving no score for his dramatic effort. Even as the rider is thrown and falling toward what will surely be a hard impact, he keeps his eyes glued to the bull to observe its motions and anticipate how and where it will move next. As soon as the rider hits the arena floor, he must get to his feet and hurry to safety.

The Perfect Score

It is a matter of debate as to whether a perfect score in bull riding should be possible. Only once has a score of 100 been awarded and that was to Wade Leslie, who rode stock contractor John Growney's bull, Wolfman, at a rodeo in Central Point, Oregon, in 1991.

If the judges decide that the bull's performance was not up to the standard of other bulls in the competition, they will award the cowboy a lower score but offer him a re-ride. The cowboy then has the option of keeping his lower score or getting on a different bull and trying for a higher score. The results of his first ride will be nullified if the bull rider opts for a re-ride. If he is bucked off on his re-ride, the cowboy gets a "no score" for the competition. Sometimes bull riders who are trying to get a greater aggregate, or collective, score in order to qualify for a short go round will keep a lower score rather than risk a "no score" on a different, more active bull.

INTERVIEW WITH ROB BELL

Rob Bell is a three-time Canadian bull-riding champion and three-time National Finals Rodeo qualifier. He finished eleventh in the 2004 PBR standings and has twice won the Glen Keeley Award, which is given to the Canadian bull rider who has won the most prize money in the PBR. Bell began riding calves when he was two years old, eventually worked his way up to steers, and got on his first bull at a high school rodeo. At the time of this interview, Bell was twenty-six years old and had been riding bulls professionally for six years. He was interviewed by Jessica Kubke in March 2005 at the Rodeo Royal in Calgary, Alberta, Canada.

Q: How many rodeos do you enter in a year? Or in a healthy year anyway?

A: Well, the most rodeos I've ever competed at in a year were 125. I don't know. Some rodeos you get on a couple bulls, so I think I counted I got on over 200 bulls that year. And I did sit out a month that year, too—I was hurt for a month of that year.

Q: You mentioned that you go to the gym and work out. Is that what you do to train?

A: Yeah. I don't get on bulls for practice. I've never ever been on a bull for practice, just because you can't tell the bull that it's just practice: "OK, you can't step on me today or run me over because this is just practice!" You know, that just doesn't work. A lot of guys do practice a lot, you know, and I've just never found the need to. I get on enough, you know, getting on three, four bulls a week. I'm sore enough as it is.

Q: Do you have a preride ritual or routine that you go through?

A: I don't. It's hard to get into a real routine because you're in a different place and getting on a different bull every time. I just like to, you know, obviously get my equipment ready, get my rope rosined, and stay loose, do some stretching beforehand and . . . right before I ride, I just try and take a few moments to myself and just try and focus. And then after that, I just crawl into the chute, and a lot of times it just goes blank from there.

Q: What are some of the serious injuries you've suffered? Or the most typical?

A: I've torn my elbow. I tore some ligaments in my elbow and that was pretty bad—I missed eight months with that. I had surgery on it. Broken ribs—I broke three ribs earlier this year, two ribs two years

Canadian bull rider Rob Bell of Houston, British Columbia, Canada, is shoved by the bull's head following an unsuccessful ride at the Calgary Stampede on July 14, 2001. Bell would also be tossed into the air by this bull immediately after this photograph was taken, but he sustained no injuries. The Stampede, billed as "The Greatest Outdoor Show on Earth," is held every July in Calgary, Alberta, Canada. It began in 1886 as an agricultural exhibition to which the rodeo was added in 1912. Today, it is a ten-day rodeo and celebration of Western Canadian heritage that attracts more than a million visitors from around the world and offers millions of dollars in prize money.

ago. Bruised my liver. Bruised my lungs. I've had . . . I wouldn't even be able to start to know how many concussions I've had. Um, broke my nose a few times. Broke my arm. Tore my groin—that was probably the most painful out of all of them.

Q: What safety equipment would you never ride without?

A: My vest. When I started riding bulls, we didn't have vests. Because I started in '94 and that's kind of when they started to come around, and I was one of the first guys in Canada, in British Columbia anyway, to get a vest, and every rodeo five or six guys would borrow it for that first year. And the next year guys started to have them. But I mean, when I started . . . I could only imagine, but I would almost guarantee I wouldn't be riding bulls right now, and I might not be alive if it hadn't been for my vest . . . all the times I've been stepped on in the chest and horns I've got in the chest. Surely it would have broken my ribs and done some internal injuries. I don't know, but I think that vest may have saved my life before. I just very rarely see anyone ride without one anymore.

Q: In your mind, what makes a good bull rider, both physically and mentally?

A: Well, physically you just have to be in shape. I mean, the physical part of bull riding is probably 30 percent . . . it's probably 70 percent mental and 30 percent physical. With the breeding they're doing on the bulls now, the bulls are getting a lot tougher. I've noticed a huge change just since I've started. You know, they artificially inseminate these cows and I mean they're . . . they got bloodlines and it's all down on paper [from whom these bulls are descended]. But it used to be they just went to stockyards and looked at the bull and, well, "we'll try him," and they try him out, and he might buck a little bit, but now there's a science to it. So it's a lot more physically demanding now than it was even when I started. I'm twenty-six now, and I feel like I'm getting old to be a bull rider. I really have to work at going to the gym and trying to stay in shape, where I never used to have to work at it when I was starting out. But now I notice that the bulls have so much more power.

Q: When do you see yourself leaving the sport?

A: A lot of that depends on injuries. I might be done tomorrow. But I don't want to ride bulls past thirty-five.

Q: What is your favorite thing about being a bull rider?

A: Just the free lifestyle . . . traveling all around the country. How many twenty-six-year-olds do you know that can drive from here to Miami without a map? I can drive from here to Los Angeles without a map, here to New York, anywhere . . . I know the country. I can drive around Houston, Dallas, L.A., you know, anywhere without a map. I've just been around the country, and it's just fun.

CONCLUSION

The world's best bull riders have come in different sizes and have come to bull riding by many different avenues, but the one thing they have all had in common is that rare quality cowboys call "try." It takes a lot of guts to get on a bull, and, while most people wouldn't dream of doing it, bull riders wouldn't dream of doing anything else. The money to be made riding bulls has increased dramatically over the years, but the world's top bull riders have never been in it for the money. They ride bulls because they love it. Ty Murray, the first cowboy in history to pass the million-dollar mark in rodeo winnings, claims in his book *King of the Cowboys: The Autobiography of the World's Most Famous Rodeo Star*: "I'd do this for nothing. That's how I got started, and it's why I do it today." Few sports demand that so much strength, determination, endurance, and courage be packed into a mere eight seconds of intense exertion. Bull riding is an event like no other, and bull riders are truly one-of-a-kind in their competitive spirit and ability. For as long as there are bulls to ride, there will be cowboys who will try to ride them and an audience eager to watch.

List of Champions

Below is a list of the PRCA world champion bull riders from 1929 to 2004.

PRCA CHAMPIONS

NAME	RESIDENCE	YEAR
John Schneider	Livermore, CA	1929–1930
Smokey Snyder	Bellflower, CA	1931
John Schneider	Livermore, CA (tie)	1932
Smokey Snyder	Bellflower, CA (tie)	1932
Frank Schneider	Caliente, CA	1933–1934
Smokey Snyder	Bellflower, CA	1935–1937
Kid Fletcher	Hugo, CO	1938
Dick Griffith	Fort Worth, TX	1939–1942
Ken Roberts	Strong City, KA	1943–1945
Pee Wee Morris	Custer, SD	1946
Wag Blesing	Bell, CA	1947
Harry Tompkins	Dublin, TX	1948–1950
Jim Shoulders	Henryetta, OK	1951
Harry Tompkins	Dublin, TX	1952
Todd Whatley	Hugo, OK	1953
Jim Shoulders	Henryetta, OK	1954–1959
Harry Tompkins	Dublin, TX	1960
Ronnie Rossen	Broadus, MT	1961
Freckles Brown	Lawton, OK	1962
Bill Kornell	Palm Springs, CA	1963
Bob Wegner	Auburn, WA	1964
Larry Mahan	Brooks, OR	1965
Ronnie Rossen	Broadus, MT	1966

List of Champions

NAME	RESIDENCE	YEAR
Larry Mahan	Brooks, OR	1967
George Paul	Del Rio, TX	1968
Doug Brown	Silverton, OR	1969
Gary Leffew	Santa Maria, CA	1970
Bill Nelson	San Francisco, CA	1971
John Quintana	Creswell, OR	1972
Bobby Steiner	Austin, TX	1973
Don Gay	Mesquite, TX	1974–1977
Butch Kirby	Alba, TX	1978
Don Gay	Mesquite, TX	1979–1981
Charles Sampson	Los Angeles, CA	1982
Cody Snyder	Redcliff, Alberta	1983
Don Gay	Mesquite, TX	1984
Ted Nuce	Manteca, CA	1985
Tuff Hedeman	Gainesville, TX	1986
Lane Frost	Lane, OK	1987
Jim Sharp	Kermit, TX	1988
Tuff Hedeman	Bowie, TX	1989
Jim Sharp	Kermit, TX	1990
Tuff Hedeman	Bowie, TX	1991
Cody Custer	Wickenburg, AZ	1992
Ty Murray	Stephenville, TX	1993
Daryl Mills	Pink Mountain, British Columbia	1994
Jerome Davis	Archdale, NC	1995
Terry Don West	Henryetta, OK	1996
Scott Mendes	Weatherford, TX	1997
Ty Murray	Stephenville, TX	1998

NAME	RESIDENCE	YEAR
Mike White	Lake Charles, LA	1999
Cody Hancock	Taylor, AZ	2000
Blue Stone	Ogden, UT	2001–2002
Terry Don West	Henryetta, OK	2003
Dustin Elliott	Tecumseh, NE	2004

Below is a list of the PRCA World Champion bull riders from 1994 to 2004.

PBR CHAMPIONS

NAME	RESIDENCE	YEAR
Adriano Moraes	Sao Paulo, Brazil	1994
Tuff Hedeman	Morgan Mill, TX	1995
Owen Washburn	Lordsburg, NM	1996
Michael Gaffney	Albuquerque, NM	1997
Troy Dunn	Sarina, Australia	1998
Cody Hart	Gainesville, TX	1999
Chris Shivers	Jonesville, LA	2000
Adriano Moraes	Sao Paulo, Brazil	2001
Ednei Caminhas	Sao Paulo, Brazil	2002
Chris Shivers	Jonesville, LA	2003
Mike Lee	Alvord, TX	2004

Glossary

bronc Short for "bronco"; a horse that has not been fully "broken," or trained to be ridden. In a rodeo, "bronc" refers to horses used in bronc-riding competitions, in which a rider must stay on the horse's back for eight seconds while it attempts to buck him off.

bull rope A flat-woven rope that goes around the chest of the bull. The cowboy puts his riding hand palm-upward into a handhold in this rope, which sits atop the bull, and then binds the tail of the rope around his hand.

droppy A term used to describe a bull that kicks his back legs while his front legs are still off the ground.

eliminator Referring to a bull considered impossible to ride and, hence, on which to score.

hook A bull hitting a cowboy or bullfighter with its horns.

hung up Referring to a cowboy who has been bucked off the bull, but whose riding hand has not come out of the wrap. Being "hung up" is the cause of many serious injuries in bull riding.

purse The amount of prize money that will be awarded at a particular rodeo.

rank Referring to a bull that is difficult to stay on but for that reason can be ridden for a high score.

rosin A waxy substance that comes in small, rocklike form, which bull riders rub into their ropes and gloves to prevent slipping.

rowels The spiked disks on a cowboy's spur. Bull riders dull their rowels and fix them in place in order to better hang on to the bull with their feet.

short go round The final cycle of competition in a rodeo event, in which only the cowboys who have earned the highest scores in earlier rounds ride (sometimes simply called the "short go").

steer A young male that has not yet matured into an adult bull.

try The amount of effort and grit a cowboy demonstrates in staying on a bull.

well Going "into the well" refers to a cowboy being drawn into the center of a bull's spin by centrifugal force.

wrap The rope that binds the bull rider's hand to the handhold. A bull rider "takes his wrap" as he binds his hand into the bull rope handle. To "pull the wrap" is to pull the tail end of the bull rope to release the rider's hand after his ride.

wreck When the bull and cowboy collide, potentially resulting in injury, or when the cowboy is thrown from the bull and injured.

For More Information

National Cowboy & Western Heritage Museum
1700 NE 63rd Street
Oklahoma City, OK 73111
(405) 478-2250
Web site: http://www.nationalcowboymuseum.org

National High School Rodeo Association, Inc.
12001 Tejon Street, Suite 128
Denver, CO 80234
(303) 452-0820
Web site: http://www.nhsra.org

National Little Britches Rodeo Association
1045 W. Rio Grande
Colorado Springs, CO 80906
(719) 389-0333
Web site: http://www.nlbra.com

Professional Bull Riders, Inc. (PBR)
6 South Tejon Street, Suite 700
Colorado Springs, CO 80903
(719) 471-3008
Web site: http://www.pbrnow.com

Professional Rodeo Cowboys Association (PRCA)
101 ProRodeo Drive
Colorado Springs, CO 80919-2301
(719) 593-8840
Website: http://www.prorodeo.org

ProRodeo Hall of Fame & Museum of the American Cowboy
101 ProRodeo Drive
Colorado Springs, CO 80919
(719) 528-4761
Website: http://www.prorodeo.com

WEB SITES

Due to the changing nature of Internet links, the Rosen Publishing Group, Inc., has developed an online list of Web sites related to the subject of this book. This site is updated regularly. Please use this link to access the list:

http://www.rosenlinks.com/woro/buri

For Further Reading

Annerino, John. *Roughstock: The Toughest Events in Rodeo*. New York, NY: Four Walls Eight Windows, 2000.

Barwick, Lyle, and Laura Shay Lynes. *Rodeo, 1990–2000: The Last Ten Years*. Calgary, AB: Ion Publishing, 2000.

Johnson, Dirk. *Biting the Dust: The Wild Ride and Dark Romance of the Rodeo Cowboy and the American West*. New York, NY: Simon & Schuster, 1994.

Mellis, Allison Fuss. *Riding Buffaloes and Broncos: Rodeo and Native Traditions in the Northern Great Plains*. Norman, OK: University of Oklahoma Press, 2003.

Russell, Don. *The Wild West; or, A History of the Wild West Shows*. Fort Worth, TX: Amon Carter Museum of Western Art, 1970.

Wooden, Wayne S. *Rodeo in America: Wranglers, Roughstock and Paydirt*. Lawrence, KS: University Press of Kansas, 1996.

Bibliography

Amateur Bull Rider. "Bull Riding Equipment." Retrieved February 11, 2005 (http://members.tripod.com/~Scout0057/equip_info.htm).

Barris, Ted. *Rodeo Cowboys: The Last Heroes*. Edmonton, AB: Executive Sport Publications, 1981.

Campion, Lynn. *Rodeo: Behind the Scenes at America's Most Exciting Sport.* Guilford, CT: Lyons Press, 2002.

Coplon, Jeff. *Gold Buckle: The Grand Obsession of Rodeo Bull Riders*. New York, NY: HarperCollins West, 1995.

Cowan, Floyd. *Bull Riding: Rodeo's Most Dangerous 8 Seconds*. Calgary, AB: Detselig Enterprises, 1999.

Eamer, Claire. *The Canadian Rodeo Book*. Saskatoon, SK: Western Producer Prairie Books, 1982.

For Frost Enterprises. "Quotes." Retrieved May 2005 (http://www.lanefrost.com/quotes.htm).

Fredriksson, Kristine. *American Rodeo: From Buffalo Bill to Big Business*. College Station, TX: Texas A&M University Press, 1985.

Handbook of Texas Online. "Rodeos." Retrieved February 11, 2005 (http://www.tsha.utexas.edu/handbook/online/articles/view/RR/llr1.html).

Lawrence, Elizabeth Atwood. *Rodeo: An Anthropologist Looks at the Wild and the Tame*. Knoxville, TN: University of Tennessee Press, 1982.

LeCompte, Mary Lou. *Cowgirls of the Rodeo: Pioneer Professional Athletes*. Urbana, IL: University of Illinois Press, 1993.

McDonald, Bryan. "Xtreme Bulls—San Antonio Notes." January 31, 2003. Retrieved December 29, 2004 (http://probullstats.com/23xtras/bulltour_sanatone.htm).

Murray, Ty. *King of the Cowboys: The Autobiography of the World's Most Famous Rodeo Star*. New York, NY: Atria Books, 2003.

National Cowboy & Western Heritage Museum. "American Rodeo Gallery." Retrieved January 8, 2005 (http://www.nationalcowboymuseum.org/g_rode_info.html).

Bull Riding

Poulsen, David A. *Wild Ride! Three Journeys Down the Rodeo Road.* Toronto, ON: Balmur Book Publishing, 2000.

Santos, Kendra. *Ring of Fire: The Guts and Glory of the Professional Bull Riders Tour.* Chicago, IL: Triumph Books, 2000.

Savitt, Sam. *Rodeo: Cowboys, Bulls, and Broncos.* Garden City, NY: Doubleday, 1963.

Thieme, Trevor. Men's Health. Profile of Gary Leffew. August 2004. Retrieved May 2005 (http://www.menshealth.com/cda/article.do?site=MensHealth&channel=fitness&conitem=233a99edbbbd201099edbbbd2010cfe793cd____).

2005 Media Guide. Colorado Springs, CO: Professional Bull Riders, 2005.

"Warriors of the Rainbow Rodeo." *California Heartland Special Edition* Program 756. Produced by Patiricia McConahay for California Heartland Television. Broadcast in 2005.

Woerner, Gail Hughbanks. *Fearless Funnymen: The History of the Rodeo Clown.* Austin, TX: Eakin Press, 1993.

Woerner, Gail Hughbanks. "How the Cowboy Turtle Association Began." Rodeoattitude.com. Retrieved January 24, 2005 (http://www.rodeoattitude.com/dir/_hd/gail/past_7.htm).

Index

B

Bell, Rob, interview with, 31–35
Boston Garden Rodeo, 9
Branger, Clint, 17
bull rider, build for, 15, 34
bulls
  riding, 25–28
  types of, 11

C

Calgary Stampede, 7
Cheyenne Frontier Days, 7, 20
Cody, Buffalo Bill, 6
Cowboys' Turtle Association, 9, 13

E

earnings, 8–9, 13, 36
equipment, 21–22, 28, 34

F

Frost, Lane, 17, 19–20

G

Griffith, Dick, 16

H

Hedeman, Tuff, 17–18

I

injuries, 19, 20, 28, 32–34

J

judging, 29–31

L

Lambert, Cody, 17, 20, 28
Leffew, Gary, 15

M

Madison Square Garden Rodeo, 16
Murray, Ty, 17, 36

N

National Finals Rodeo, 31
National High School Rodeo Association (NHSRA), 11
National Intercollegiate Rodeo Association (NIRA), 11

O

101 Ranch Show, 6

P

Pendleton Round-Up, 7
preparation, 22–23
Prescott Frontier Days, 7
Pro Bull Riders (PBR), 13–14, 28, 31
Professional Rodeo Cowboys Association (PRCA), 9, 14
purses/prizes, 7, 9, 13, 14, 18, 31

R

Roberts, Ken, 16
rodeo, history of, 6–11
Rodeo Association of America (RAA), 8, 13
rodeo clowns, 11–13

Rodeo Cowboys Association, 9
rules, 9, 21

S

Sampson, Charles, 18–19
Schneider, Frank, 16
Schneider, John, 16
Sharp, Jim, 17
Shoulders, Jim, 16, 17
Snyder, Smokey, 16

T

Tompkins, Harry, 16–17

W

Wild West shows, 6, 7, 16
Women's Professional Rodeo Association (WPRA), 11

X

Xtreme Bulls, 14

ABOUT THE AUTHORS

Jessica and Jane Kubke grew up in Calgary, Alberta, the center of ranching and rodeo in Canada. The sisters learned to ride horses as girls and grew up attending rodeos. They got truly hooked on bull riding in the course of their first jobs at the Calgary Stampede, one of the world's oldest and most venerated rodeos. From behind the chutes, they have been close enough to the action to taste the dirt while watching luminaries like Lane Frost, Charles Sampson, Tuff Hedeman, and Ty Murray get on rank bulls. They have watched countless qualified rides and wrecks since and never miss the Calgary Stampede or the Canadian Finals Rodeo.

PHOTO CREDITS

Cover, pp. 1, 26 © David Stoecklein/Corbis; pp. 4–5 © SuperStock Inc./SuperStock; pp. 7, 8 Library of Congress Prints and Photographs Division; p. 9 (inset) Wyoming State Archives, Department of State Parks and Cultural Resources; p. 10 © Yann Arthus-Bertrand/Corbis; p. 12 © Larry Proser/SuperStock; p. 13 © Professional Bull Riders; p. 16 © Hulton-Deutsch Collection/Corbis; p. 17 Time-Life Pictures/Getty Images; pp. 18, 30 © AP/Wide World Photos; p. 19 © Mark Allen Johnson/ZUMA/Corbis; p. 20 © Andre Jenny/The Image Works; p. 22 © Jeff Greenberg/The Image Works; p. 23 © SuperStock, Inc./SuperStock; p. 24 © Sean Cayton/The Image Works; p. 27 © Arlene Collins/The Image Works; p. 33 © Reuters/Corbis.

Designer: Les Kanturek